RISE OF
ZOMBERT

Y-91

RISE OF
ZOMBERT

Kara LaReau
illustrated by Ryan Andrews

CANDLEWICK PRESS

Text copyright © 2020 by Kara LaReau
Illustrations copyright © 2020 by Ryan Andrews

First edition 2020

Library of Congress Catalog Card Number pending
ISBN 978-1-5362-0106-2

20 21 22 23 24 25 LSC 10 9 8 7 6 5 4 3 2 1

Printed in Crawfordsville, IN, U.S.A.

This book was typeset in ITC Mendoza Roman.
The illustrations were created digitally.

Candlewick Press
99 Dover Street
Somerville, Massachusetts 02144

visit us at www.candlewick.com

A JUNIOR LIBRARY GUILD SELECTION

*For Lullabye, Josie, Bunny, Gatsby, Oscar,
Louis, Scully, Pearl, and Sugar*

K. L.

For Ella and Lily

R. A.

CHAPTER ONE

It was a cold fall night in the town of Lambert, and the moon was full. The only sounds were the buzzing of the streetlamps and the scattering of dead leaves across the windy, empty streets . . . and, in a lab on the outskirts of town, the creak of a cage door.

A shadowy figure emerged from that cage. Bloodied and frail, he slunk through the room, sniffing the air. He would have to be quick; the assistant on duty had left the lab and could be back at any moment. The inhabitants of the other cages looked on encouragingly.

I'll come back for you, he seemed to tell them. *I promise.*

As he scrambled away through an air duct, those who remained behind were silent. They wanted to give at least one of their number the best chance of escape.

The shadowy figure made his way through the maze of the air-duct system, sniffing all the way, until he found where it vented to the outside. Using his remaining energy, he jumped. The air outside was

crisp and cold, not stale like it was in the lab, and he let it fill his lungs. He assessed the fence, which he thought he'd need to scale, but then he saw the hole. It was a good-size hole, so he'd have no problem getting through.

The problem was that he was weak. So weak. He hadn't eaten in a couple of days; he couldn't stomach the food they'd been giving him, which was too soft and smelled wrong and didn't have any crunchy bones or pulsing blood in it. Food always tasted better when you caught it and killed it yourself, and it had been a long time since he'd been able to hunt the way he liked. Too long. But he needed energy now.

He saw the dumpster, which was too tall for him to jump into in his condition. But then he saw the barrel. He sniffed and smelled something that just might be food. He had no energy left to jump, so all he could do was let himself fall, and then land — amid nothing but empty cans and bottles and other trash. He had failed, he thought. And then he passed out.

Eventually, the lab assistant returned and finished the remainder of his shift. The sun had begun to rise over Lambert, and the empty cage marked Y-91 wouldn't be noticed until later that morning.

CHAPTER TWO

*E*verybody say *frittata!*" my dad said.

"ITTATA!" yelled Emmett.

"ITTATA! ITTATA!" yelled Ezra, clapping his hands.

Dad circled around the table, taking video of the twins with his phone. I covered my face.

"Come on, Mellie," he said. "Don't you want to be in this one? I'm thinking of calling it 'Sunday Fun-Day Breakfast.'"

I shook my head. I knew Mom and Dad wanted me to want to participate; after all, their blog was called *Family, Food, and Fun.*

"Mellie, don't touch the bacon yet," my mother said.

"But I'm *hungry*," I said. I groaned and held my stomach for maximum effect.

"Well, I'm still trying to get a photo," Mom said, adjusting her camera lens. "This light just isn't right."

"Maybe you need the reflector," my father suggested.

"Good idea!" Mom said.

As she ran off to get it, my father finally sat down.

"So," he said. "Any big plans for today?"

"Danny and I are going to hang out," I said. "And I still need to pick a topic for my presentation."

We were studying organisms at school, and everyone in my class was supposed to do an oral report on a living thing.

"Do you have any ideas yet?" my father asked.

"I have a whole list," I said, pulling it out of the pocket of my favorite coveralls, where I'd put it so I could share it with Danny later. "Garden slug, millipede, flying squirrel, sea urchin, vampire bat, Portuguese man-of-war, Komodo dragon, duck-billed platypus . . . "

"That's quite a menagerie," my father said.

"I want to pick something unique," I explained.

"Unique, like you," my father said, ruffling my hair.

"*You*-neek!" shouted Emmett.

"Neek! Neek!" shouted Ezra.

My father grabbed his phone, hit video, and pointed it at the twins. "Ooh, can you two say that again?" he asked.

"Time to photograph some bacon!" my mother said, returning with the reflector.

Unfortunately, my parents seemed more interested in cooking and photographing our food than actually eating it, which meant I hadn't had a hot meal in more than two years. They started blogging when they were trying to have another baby, and then they really got into it when they adopted the twins. Dad used to be a chef and Mom used to be a freelance writer, but when the blog took off, they quit their jobs. Now this was all they did, full-time.

That morning, I managed to eat a few bites of cold frittata and gulp down my orange juice.

"May I be excused?" I asked.

But my parents were too busy trying to get Emmett and Ezra to sing a song about bacon and eggs. It was a song they used to sing to me at breakfast, before the twins came along. I put my plate in the dishwasher and headed for the door.

"I'm going to meet Danny!" I shouted. As if anyone really cared.

Soon after that, I was lying in a pool of blood.

Okay, actually, it was fake blood—Danny makes it himself using his own special recipe. It's supposed to be edible, but it grosses me out too much to taste it. And I was lying *near* it more than *in* it, since it grosses me out too much to touch it. Danny says I should get used to it, since I want to be a scientist, but I have plenty of time to be grossed out before that happens.

I suppose you could say we were trespassing. But when Danny and I found a hole in the back fence at the YummCo Foods factory, we took it as an invitation. Danny was the one who insisted on filming there. I thought the town cemetery or the woods behind my house would be better settings for a horror movie, but since we'd found the hole in the fence a few months before, Danny had been obsessed with filming at the factory. He thought it would make a great horror movie set, since it's at the edge of town and is big and white with tiny windows — the kind of place where evil scientists might conduct secret experiments. And set into the hill above the factory is the old mansion where Stuart Yumm, the CEO of YummCo, lives. Danny is obsessed with horror movies, and he's always "scouting for locations," as he puts it. He even has his own online channel called Hurlvision, though he doesn't have too many viewers. Danny said it takes time to build up a fan base.

Anyway, I was lying on the pavement of the loading dock behind a dumpster; we made sure to position me so Danny could get some good footage without anyone seeing us. As Danny filmed, YummCo Foods workers in their trademark brown-and-green uniforms were loading boxes and yelling to one another from inside and outside the factory.

"Your mask is crooked," Danny said.

This was the only way I'd agreed to be on

camera—if I could cover my face. Danny made the mask out of papier-mâché and painted it to look like a ghoul, with red eyes and fangs. That's the name of the movie he was making: *Gone Ghoul*.

It was just as I was trying to adjust the mask that I heard the noise.

"Mrow."

"Did you hear that?" I asked.

"What?" Danny said.

I thought it was my own stomach, seeing as it was squeezed between the dumpster and the brick wall of the factory. Also, it was almost lunchtime. Then I heard it again.

"Mrow."

"I think it's coming from inside," I said. "Help me with this."

Danny and I lifted the dumpster lid.

"Gaah!" he said. All we saw and smelled was garbage. We tried to let go of the lid gently, but it still hit the dumpster with a *CLANG*.

We looked around to see if anyone noticed, but no one did. The YummCo workers were still loading and unloading, like robots.

"Mrooooooooow."

"Okay, now I hear it," Danny admitted.

"It's not coming from the dumpster," I said. It was coming from a big blue recycling barrel next to the dumpster. I looked inside.

At first, I just saw two pale-yellow eyes. I squinted and leaned in, and the eyes became part of a head, and the head became part of a cat. And it wasn't just any cat.

It was the ugliest cat I'd ever seen.

Danny peered down into the barrel, too. "What is that?" he asked.

"It's a cat," I said. "I think."

"Mroooow."

"Well, it sounds like a cat," Danny said. "What's it doing here?"

"Do you want to ask him?" I said. Danny made a face.

"MROOOOOOOOOOW."

There was something about the cat's crying that really got to me. It's like it needed me. I stretched out my arms.

"You shouldn't do that," Danny warned. "You're

not supposed to touch stray animals. That cat could have rabies."

"Relax," I said. "It's harmless. And wow . . . skinny."

Skinny was an understatement. The cat was just skin and bones. I lifted him up out of the barrel to get a better look. It was even worse in the sunlight. He (with a quick look, I could tell it was a he) was missing a lot of the fur on his stomach and legs, and the fur that remained was matted and dull. He had some dried blood on what was left of his ear, probably from a recent catfight. And he smelled almost as bad as the dumpster.

"Yuck," Danny said.

But as soon as I pulled the cat out of the recycling barrel, he started purring. He put a paw on either side of my neck and leaned his head on my chest. It was like he was trying to hug me. If it wasn't for the smell, I would have tried to hug him back.

"It's okay," I told him. "We need to get you cleaned up."

"So . . . wait. You're going to keep this thing?" Danny asked.

"This 'thing' is a cat. And yes, I'm going to keep him," I said.

Danny scoffed. "What are you going to name him? Fleabag? Mr. Bones? Stinky?"

I looked at the blue barrel. On the outside, it said:

PROPERTY OF

TOWN OF

LAMBERT

"Bert," I decided, looking into the cat's yellow eyes. "Your name will be Bert."

And then I zipped Bert into my hoodie, got on my bike, and started pedaling. Eventually, Danny caught up.

CHAPTER THREE

It was Kari who noticed the empty cage, when she took inventory at the beginning of her shift that morning.

"Huh," Greg said, jiggling the latch. "I guess a screw was loose."

"When *I* lock the cages, I always double-check," Kari informed him. She tried to look serious as she said it, but inside, she was giddy. She'd been waiting and hoping for Greg to make a mistake since he was hired a few months ago. When he didn't, she'd decided to take matters (and a screwdriver) into her own hands. Now that promotion to senior lab assistant would be hers, she just knew it.

Greg and the lab animals looked on as Kari put on gloves and examined the interior of the cage.

"Looks like it ripped off its tracking tag, too. And part of his ear along with it," she said.

"Ugh," Greg said. "How much trouble do you think I'm in?"

"It doesn't matter what *I* think," Kari said. She took off her gloves with a snap and tossed them into the trash. "You need to tell the Big Boss."

At the sound of the Big Boss's name, the animals began whimpering and pawing at their cages.

"The B-Big Boss?" Greg said.

"Don't worry," Kari said, smiling. "I'll go with you. We lab assistants need to stick together, right?"

"We can't have Y-91 out in the world!" the Big Boss bellowed. "We have no idea what it's capable of!"

"I've searched everywhere in the lab," said Kari. "No sign of it. And without its tracking tag, we're at a loss."

"Of course, I take full responsibility," Greg noted, hanging his head. Kari was surprised he didn't mention the faulty latch; she definitely would have.

"I should fire you," the Big Boss harrumphed. "But I admire those who take responsibility for their mistakes. As long as they're willing to make it right."

"I am," said Greg. "I'll do anything."

What? If Kari had screwed up like this, she knew she'd have been fired. But Greg got to stay? Getting rid of him was going to be harder than she expected.

"I'm surprised Y-91 had the strength to escape. Its stats had dropped considerably over the past few days," Kari said, showing the Big Boss the latest test results. "Actually, I thought it'd be a goner this morning when I checked its cage."

"*You're* responsible for finding it," the Big Boss said, pointing a finger at Greg, then looking at Kari. "But *you're* in charge."

Kari nodded. She was in charge. She liked the sound of that.

"I'll get a hazmat team together to search the grounds," she said. "If we don't find it, we'll come up with a new plan."

"Don't worry. We won't let you down," said Greg.

"You won't let me down *again*," the Big Boss growled.

CHAPTER FOUR

When we got Bert back to my house, the first thing we did was to give him a bath in the backyard. We filled up my brothers' plastic wading pool with water from the hose, and I used some of my mom's fancy shampoo, which smells like roses.

You'd think it would be hard to bathe a cat—from what I've heard, they don't like water the way dogs do. But Bert stayed perfectly relaxed.

"He looks almost limp," Danny noted.

"I bet he's just miserable from being so dirty and stinky," I said. "This bath is probably a big relief."

"Are your parents going to let you keep him?" Danny asked as we dried Bert with a towel.

"Probably not," I said. "Which is why I'm not going to tell them about him."

"You won't get away with that for long," Danny said.

"Longer than you'd think," I said. "My parents aren't like your mom. Unless it's about *Family, Food, and Fun*, they don't notice anything. Or any*one*."

"That's true," Danny said.

We unwrapped Bert from the towel and took a look. He seemed cleaner, but his patches of fur were still dull and clumpy. And he still smelled, though not as much as before. Now he smelled like garbage *and* roses.

"Mroooow!"

At least one of us thought it was an improvement.

After we cleaned up, Danny and I wrapped Bert in the towel again and went inside my house. "The Hokey Pokey" was blaring, and the twins were having a dance party while my father was capturing the whole thing on video. My mom was sitting at the dining room table with the laptop, probably posting photos of frittata and bacon on the blog. They all looked so happy together . . . without me. Of course, no one even noticed us as we walked by them and up the stairs.

Danny held Bert while I did my best to cat-proof my room. First, I put away all my books and art supplies. Then I moved all my science experiments to my highest shelf; my studies of static electricity and centrifugal force and liquid chromatography would have to wait. Finally, I pulled out my old purple beanbag chair and smooshed it in the center.

"Now you have a place to sleep," I informed Bert. Instead, he wriggled out of Danny's arms and went into one of the baskets under my bed, where he made his own Bert-size nest out of a bunch of my old stuffed animals. Almost instantly, he was asleep.

"I guess he doesn't like purple," Danny said.

"Well, that makes two of us," I said. "Now we need to go to the library. And the pet store."

"For what?" Danny asked.

"I need books on cats," I said. "And we need food and supplies for Bert."

"Can't you look it up online?" Danny asked, motioning to the phone tucked into my coveralls.

Even though we're only nine, Danny and I have our own phones, because his mom works a lot and my mom and dad are big fans of free-range parenting, which means I get to go wherever I want by myself, as long as I tell them where I'm going and what I'm doing and "use my head." It's supposed to encourage me to function independently. You'd think having phones would make us look cool to the other kids in the fourth grade — unfortunately, we seem uncool in too many other ways.

"My parents disabled just about everything, remember? I can only use it to make emergency calls and take photos and play a few boring games," I reminded him. "And my mom is never far from our laptop, in case she needs to post something."

"You can use my phone to look stuff up," he offered.

"I hate reading on yours. It gives me a headache," I said.

"All right, then. The library it is," Danny said. "Though this is really going to affect my filming schedule."

"We can do more filming one day after school this week. But for now, Bert needs us," I said.

I leaned under the bed.

"Hey, Bert," I whispered. "Danny and I are going out for a little while. But we'll be back soon with some cat stuff for you. Okay?"

All I heard was wheezy snoring. I took that as a yes.

"Danny and I are going to the library, then to the store!" I shouted as we ran out the door.

"Be back in time for dinner — I'm making something special!" my dad yelled. The twins were still dancing around while my parents were editing their "Hokey Pokey" video.

The YummCo Memorial Library is on the other

side of town, near YummCo Incorporated, the corporate office where Danny's mom works. Just about everything in Lambert has something to do with YummCo. Our school is named YummCo Elementary, and our colors are brown and green, too.

Even though I had to get some cat books, I don't need an excuse to go to the library. I like being around all the books, even the big display they have at the front featuring Stuart Yumm's autobiography (*Yumm Luck*) and his book of business advice (*Yumm Sense*) and a cookbook by his daughter, Yolanda (*Yumm in Your Tumm*). I like the way library books smell: old and a little musty. And I really like the librarian in the children's room, Ms. Michiko. She knows just about everything about everything. And she always wears interesting earrings in the shapes of books or shoes or animals. That day she was actually wearing cat earrings. I took that as a sign.

"Cats were considered sacred in some ancient societies," Ms. Michiko informed us after I told her what I needed. "In Egypt, some cats were mummified after death, just like humans."

"Mummified?" Danny said. "Cool!"

"The Greek historian Herodotus wrote that when a cat died, its human family would often shave their eyebrows in mourning," Ms. Michiko added.

I nodded. I was glad I didn't live in an ancient society. I'd look pretty weird without eyebrows.

She walked us over to the shelves filled with animal books. "Most of the cat books are out on loan right now. But it looks like we have three available."

Those three turned out to be *The Kids Book of Kitties, Fearless Felines,* and *The Cat Book.* The first one was too babyish, and the second one was just pictures of cats playing the piano or riding on dogs. So we had to settle for *The Cat Book.*

Bert was still under my bed when we got home.

"It looks like he drank some water," Danny noted, inspecting the bowl as I set up Bert's litter box in my closet.

"Well, hopefully he'll eat some of this food," I said. "If not, I just wasted all the money in my microscope fund."

For months, I'd been saving for a real,

laboratory-grade microscope I saw in the latest *KidScience!* catalog. It had glass optics and dual LED illumination and everything, and it came with slides and forceps and test tubes, and even a petri dish, perfect for all the diseases I was hoping to cure. Unfortunately, it turned out cat food was expensive, especially the good kind that had actual meat in it.

I scooped the contents of a can of YummCo Organic Kitty Superfood onto a dish and gently pushed it under the bed. It didn't smell very good, but maybe that's because I wasn't a cat. Bert looked down at the dish, then looked back at me and Danny.

"Bon appétit," I said.

Danny took out his phone and started filming.

"Cut it out," I said.

"What?" Danny asked. "A mutant cat is just what my movie needs."

"We should give him some privacy," I suggested. My parents were always trying to film me when I ate, and I didn't like it one bit.

"Well, what do you want to do now?" Danny

asked, putting his phone away. "We could go to the woods and do some more filming for *Gone Ghoul,* or hang out at my house."

"I think I'm just going to stay here and read," I said. "And hang out with Bert."

"Okay," Danny said. He pulled a stack of books and comics out of his backpack and flopped down on the purple beanbag. When you're really good friends like me and Danny, each person is cool with whatever the other one wants to do, even if it means not really doing anything.

While Danny read *The Filmmaker's Eye* and *Making Monster Movies,* I spent the afternoon reading *The Cat Book.* It was actually pretty interesting; among other things, I learned that cats have a layer of cells behind their retinas that help them see at night, and that they have better hearing than dogs.

I paid special attention to the chapter on cat health. Healthy cats are supposed to have bright eyes and shiny fur; Bert's eyes were definitely bright, but the fur he did have was pretty . . . mangy. Was he sick?

I looked under the bed; Bert was still there, and so

was his YummCo Organic Kitty Superfood. He hadn't eaten a bite.

"Come on, cat," I said. "You must be starving."

"Maybe you need to take a bite, to show him how good it is," Danny said.

I pulled the plate out from under the bed. The food didn't look pink anymore; it was grayish and lumpy. And it didn't smell any better.

"No way," I said. "Eating cat food is where I draw the line."

Instead, I pretended to eat it. I raised the plate to my mouth and smacked my lips.

"Mmmmm, YummCo Organic Kitty Superfood," I said. "It's YummCo-yum-yum-yum!"

Bert just stared at me.

"'YummCo-yum-yum-yum'?" Danny raised an eyebrow. "You sound like the commercial."

"Ha-ha," I said.

"Mellie! Dinner!" my father called.

"I should go anyway," Danny said, checking his phone. "My mom just texted to remind me that Sunday is pizza night, and I don't want to miss it."

Danny and his mom ordered takeout just about every other day, and on the days they didn't, they ate leftovers. Whenever I asked my parents if we could get takeout, my mom always said, "No one wants to see us blog about *takeout*," and my dad said, "What? You don't like my cooking?"

That night, my dad made salmon with some kind of mustard and a bunch of herbs on top. I still had the aroma of that smelly cat food stuck in my nose, so I wasn't very hungry. Dad also made peas and this thing where he blends garlic and cauliflower and beans together and it tastes just like mashed potatoes, so I ate that. Thankfully, it even tasted good cold, which is what it was after my mother finished photographing it.

"So, what did you and Danny do today?" my father asked.

"Not much," I said, shoveling in a big forkful of garlic-cauliflower-beans so I wouldn't have to answer any more questions. I was anxious to get back upstairs to *The Cat Book* and to Bert.

"Did you do any filming for Danny's new movie?" my mom asked.

But before I could respond, Emmett and Ezra started a contest to see who could fit the most peas in his mouth, which ended with both of them laughing and dribbling peas everywhere. I had to admit, it was pretty adorable.

"Oh, this will make a perfect blog post!" my mother exclaimed as my father captured the whole thing on video. "We can call it 'Peas, Love, and Understanding'!"

"Open your mouth wider, Emmett," my father said. "Look at Daddy, Ezra! Say *peas!*"

"Peas! Peas!" Ezra yelled, clapping his hands.

As soon as they started in with their production, I could feel myself fading into the background, as usual. They were too distracted to notice when I excused myself and went back upstairs.

Before I knew it, it was bedtime, and I had finished *The Cat Book*. I put my pajamas on and brushed my teeth and called down "good night" to my parents, who were busy editing the peas video. Then I checked the plate of cat food one more time. Bert still hadn't eaten any of it. I pulled the basket out from under my bed to get a better look at him.

At first I thought he'd changed color, because he looked white . . . and fluffy. Then I saw all the animal heads around him.

"Aaa—!" I screamed, clamping a hand over my mouth so my parents wouldn't hear me.

Then I realized they weren't real animal heads. They were the heads of all of my stuffed animals, which he had bitten off. Bert still had one in his mouth, the head of a little stuffed chick.

"Mr. Peepers!" I cried. I managed to get the chick's head out of Bert's mouth and found the remains of the body. It was a good thing I knew how to sew.

"Mroooow."

"You're obviously hungry," I said. "Why won't you *eat?*"

"Mroooow."

"Are you sick?" I asked. *The Cat Book* said that cats can have all sorts of health problems if they don't get enough regular protein.

Then I had an idea. I brought the plate of cat food downstairs; I didn't even have to sneak it, since my parents were too preoccupied to notice. I scraped it into the trash and got some leftover salmon out of the fridge. I wiped off most of the mustard and herbs and put it on the plate.

"Okay," I said, sliding it under the bed. "If you won't eat this, I don't know what I'm going to do."

Bert opened his mouth a little and made a sniffing sound. I wondered if he was using his vomeronasal organ, which *The Cat Book* said was on the roof of a cat's mouth and helped process smells. Finally, he gave the salmon a tiny nibble.

"Mrooooooooooooow."

And then Bert actually pushed the plate away with his paw.

"Ugh!" I threw up my hands. "I give up!"

"Mroooow. Mroooow. Mroooow."

Bert pulled himself out from under the bed. Slowly, he went to my bedroom window. He leaned against the glass.

"You want out?" I said. "But I thought we were just starting to get to know each other. Do you really want to go already?"

He didn't even look at me; he just kept leaning.

"Okay," I said, sighing. I barely opened the window when Bert pushed his skinny body through it and disappeared into the darkness. I didn't even have a chance to say goodbye.

CHAPTER FIVE

He'd never had a name before, when he was free, before he was brought to the lab. There, they'd called him Y-91, but that was just the name of his cage. The girl called him Bert. He wasn't sure about the name, but the girl seemed like someone he could trust. She smelled like dirt and grass and a little like eggs, which was probably something she ate that day. He liked eggs, and the birds they came from.

He was in the woods, down by the river, where he could sense all sorts of delicious creatures lived. It was dark now, which was just the way he liked it when he hunted. But he was still so weak. He couldn't run the way he used to, so he just stayed very, very still. Something would cross his path soon, he hoped.

And then he heard a burbling from the water, followed by a rustling of leaves. It drew closer, and he could smell it, green and boggy, like the pond it came from. He could hear its heart beating and its low croaking as it situated itself on a log, and the thwack of its tongue as it began feasting on some flies.

He could see it there, small and slimy, its eyes bulging and blinking and unaware of the predator, however weakened, in its midst.

Soon, he would taste it. Oh, how he missed that first crunch, which was always the sweetest. The head, in particular, had always been his favorite.

CHAPTER SIX

Whenen I woke up the next morning, the first thing
I saw was the stack of cat food cans I'd bought, and
the plate with Bert's dinner on it, still uneaten. And
I saw what he'd done to Mr. Peepers and all my other
beloved, now-headless toys.

I really liked taking care of Bert, bathing him and
buying him good food and giving him a warm place
to sleep, and reading up on cats. I thought Bert liked
me, the way he'd leaned against me and purred. I
thought we might have been on our way to becoming
friends. So when he'd run out so quickly the night
before, I was sad.

But that morning, I was angry. *What a waste of my time,* I thought. Not to mention my money. I'd spent everything in my piggy bank on that food and the litter and the litter box, when I could have kept saving for that awesome microscope. And maybe it wasn't Bert's fault that I'd lost the receipt from the pet store, but I wouldn't have needed the receipt if he'd been less picky about his meals. He was an ungrateful cat, I decided, as I finished the last bite of the once-warm French toast my dad made for breakfast (which my mom filmed with the twins wearing berets and singing "Frère Jacques"). If I was going to have a pet, it would have to appreciate me.

If I could find the pet store receipt, I was going to go back and get myself a goldfish. That was my final thought as I walked out the back door on my way to school. That's when I saw the frog.

At least, I was pretty sure it was a frog. It was green and slimy, and it had webbed feet. But it didn't have a frog's head. In fact, it didn't have any head at all.

"Gaaaah!" I said, taking a step back. This was definitely not a stuffed animal. It was the real thing.

"Mroooow."

Bert was sitting under the rhododendron bush in the back corner of the yard. He was looking right at me, and he was licking his chops.

"Did you leave this for me?" I asked. I looked closer at the frog body. *If I want to be a scientist, I should get used to looking at actual blood and guts,* I thought.

"Mroooow." He licked his chops again. I wondered if he was still savoring that frog's head. *Yuck.* So much for me getting used to it.

"Well, we can't let anyone see this," I said. I found one of the twins' pail-and-shovel sets behind the garage. I dug a hole by the flower bed. Using the shovel (and definitely not my fingers), I scooped the headless frog into the bucket, then dumped it into the hole and covered it up.

"Mrooow?" Bert trotted up to me as I washed off the pail and shovel with the garden hose. He rubbed up against my leg. And then he looked up at me, like he was waiting for something.

I patted him on the head. "Oooookay," I said. "See you later."

■ ■ ■

"Gross!" Danny said, when I told him about the frog as we rode our bikes to school. "Can I film it?"

"Too late. I buried it—*because* it was gross," I informed him. And because I didn't want anyone else in my family walking out the door and stepping on it. Just the idea of stepping on a headless frog made me shudder. But Danny was fascinated.

"Maybe that's why Bert wasn't eating. Maybe he's used to hunting his own food," Danny said.

"I remember reading something about that in *The Cat Book*," I said. "Cats are *obligate carnivores,* it said. They're meant to hunt and eat other animals."

I stopped pedaling.

"What?" Danny asked, pulling over next to me.

"I just remembered something else," I said. I took *The Cat Book* out of my backpack. I'd planned to read it at lunchtime. (Every day at lunch, Danny and I sit together in the cafeteria and read. We call it the Reading and Eating Club. So far, we are the only two members, but we remain hopeful.)

I leafed through the book until I found the page. I'd read *The Cat Book* so quickly the day before, I'd barely skimmed the sidebar called "Wacky Cat

Behaviors." "It says some cats leave their kills on their owner's doorsteps. When they share like that, it's a sign they consider you family," I said.

"So Bert thinks *you're* his family?" Danny said.

"I guess so," I said. I put the book back and we both started pedaling again. In a weird way, it was nice to feel like I belonged in *someone's* family, even if they were a totally different species.

Then I remembered how Bert had looked up at me before I'd left that morning, like he was waiting for something. I felt bad that I didn't think to thank him.

"Why would he eat the head, though?" I asked.

"Maybe the head is like a delicacy to cats," Danny said. "I watched this show called *Extraordinary Eats* with my mom, and the host made something called *sweetbreads*. Do you know what sweetbreads are?"

"Um . . . I'm hoping it's bread," I said.

"Nope, and it's not sweet, either," Danny said. "It's the organs or glands of a calf or a lamb."

I made a sound like I was throwing up. "Organs or glands of a calf or a lamb?" I said. I couldn't seem to get that definition out of my head. It was gross,

and it almost kind of rhymed, which made it funny. And gross and funny is my favorite combination. For the rest of our ride to school, I kept repeating it.

"Organs or glands of a calf or a lamb. Organs or glands of a calf or a lamb."

"Cut it out!" Danny said. But he thought it was gross and funny, too. And pretty soon he was repeating it with me.

"Organs or glands of a calf or a lamb. ORGANS OR GLANDS OF A CALF OR A LAMB!"

The more we said it, and the louder we said it, the funnier it seemed to us. Until we ran into Carl Weems.

"Get a load of the *Weirdo Twins*," he said to the rest of the fourth grade, who were all lined up outside. And then Carl Weems laughed, and everyone else laughed, too. Because everyone in the fourth grade was scared of Carl Weems, except for me and Danny. Carl Weems was mean and not very smart, in my opinion. And he was definitely not funny, especially when he made fun of other kids, which was just about all the time. He called me "Gore-eyes" because of my glasses, and he called Danny "Girly Hurley" just because his hair is a little long and his voice is kind of high. And then, after Danny and I went as conjoined twins for Halloween last fall (a costume that won us first place at the annual YummCo Foods–sponsored Halloween Monster Mash), he started calling us the Weirdo Twins. I hated that being smart or different somehow meant we were weird, and I hated that being a girl was supposed to be an insult. We called Carl our "archnemesis," which is the worst kind of villain in comic books.

Carl Weems was in the same class as me and Danny, but he sat in the back. Danny and I sat in the front. We like to sit close to the teacher and the board so we don't miss anything. And of course, Danny and I like to sit together. I was glad our teacher, Mr. James, let us sit wherever we wanted, and not alphabetically, like most of the other teachers I'd had. And unlike the other teachers, he didn't make us sing along to the YummCo jingle, which played on the intercom each morning right after the Pledge of Allegiance.

That day, during our science lesson, Mr. James wrote the word *organism* on the board. Science is my favorite subject, especially this year, because we were studying living things. Last month, Mr. James brought in a box of earthworms and passed it around so we could all touch them. It was awesome.

"We talked a little bit about organisms on Friday," Mr. James said. "Remind me—what is an organism?"

Danny and I were the only ones to raise our hands, which made Carl cough and say "Geeks!" under his breath. I shot him a dirty look while Mr. James called on Danny.

"Um . . . a living thing?" Danny said.

"Yes!" said Mr. James. He got excited when he taught. This was one of the things I liked about him. I also liked his sense of humor. He wrote a different joke on the board every day. That day's said: *What does a skeleton say before he eats? BONE appétit!*

"But more specifically," Mr. James continued, "an organism is an animal, plant, or single-celled life-form."

As he wrote this on the board, I wrote it all down in my notebook. I loved taking notes. Danny did, too, but his handwriting wasn't as neat as mine, and he tended to doodle a little too much in the margins. Today, he was doodling what looked like a bunch of bacteria with googly eyes and fangs.

"Over the weekend, I asked all of you to think about what organism you'd like to study and present to the class. I can't wait to hear what you've chosen! So, let's pass the hat."

Mr. James passed around a Lambert Yumms baseball hat (our town's minor-league baseball team, sponsored by YummCo); it was filled with little folded-up pieces of paper, and each paper had a number written on it. I ended up with the number 3. Carl Weems got the number 1, which seemed to make him especially proud.

As soon as the hat started going around, I reached into my pocket to get my list of ideas. Only the list wasn't there. I'd been too busy thinking about Bert that morning to remember I'd left it in the pocket of my coveralls, which were still on my bedroom floor from the night before. Why did I decide to wear my corduroys today? Why, why, why?

"Mr. Carlton Weems . . . what's your organism going to be?" Mr. James asked.

Carl looked around, like he was waiting for all of us to die from the suspense.

"Rats," he said, finally.

I tried to remember what was on my list. *Think, Mellie, think!* But I couldn't remember a single idea. Was there something about a dragon? Or maybe a duck?

"Okaaay," Mr. James said, writing down Carl's choice. "Who's number two?"

"I am," said Owen Brown.

"It figures *Brown* would be *number two*," Carl said. Everyone in the class started giggling . . . except for me and Danny. Danny rolled his eyes. I was too busy freaking out. If I couldn't remember anything on my list, maybe I could just think of an idea right now. But there were millions of organisms to choose from. How could I just pick one?

Mr. James cleared his throat, and everyone calmed down. "What's it going to be, Owen?" he asked.

"Um . . . can I do a stegosaurus?" he asked. "Even if it's not 'living' right now?"

"You sure can," said Mr. James. "Okay, how about number three?"

If I wasn't freaking out before, I was really freaking out now. We could pick *extinct* organisms, too? The possibilities were nearly endless. If only I hadn't been so preoccupied with Bert yesterday—

"Three, are you out there?" Mr. James looked around.

"Right here," I said.

And then my brain froze. I couldn't think of a single living thing. Except for one.

"I'm going to go with . . . cats."

As soon as I said it, I regretted it. Cats . . . *really?* Could I *be* more boring? But then I already had *The Cat Book,* and I already had tons of cat facts rolling around in my brain, plus I might have an actual cat, if Bert was still there when I got home. It may not have been the most exciting topic, but it would probably be easy.

"An unexpected choice for Ms. Emmeline Gore," Mr. James said, writing it in his book. I couldn't tell if he was impressed or disappointed.

When we got to twenty, the last number in the class, it was Danny's turn. He ended up picking salmonella.

"What the heck is a salmonella?" asked Carl Weems.

Danny turned around. "It's a bacterium, which is a single-celled life-form," he informed everyone. "Salmonella gives you food poisoning. They just had to recall some YummCo Foods chicken because of it last month. My mom told me."

Mr. James smiled as he wrote down Danny's choice. I was jealous. Danny was the only one who picked a single-celled life-form, rather than an animal or a plant. Maybe I should have picked a bacterium. Or a cool plant, like a Venus flytrap. Anything seemed more interesting than a cat. Even one who considered me "family" and liked to eat frog heads, and who may or may not have been there when I got home.

CHAPTER SEVEN

The girl had buried the frog he'd left her without even tasting it! What a waste. He tried not to feel too offended. He did not understand her kind, and he guessed he never would.

After she left, he'd fallen asleep under the rhododendron bush, where he could enjoy some solitude. He didn't feel as weak as before, but he still felt tired. So tired. And so he'd slept. He dreamed of the others watching him from behind caged doors. Their eyes were yellow, like his, and desperate, and sad.

When he woke up it was the afternoon and the sun was shining. Almost immediately, he knew something was wrong. Well, not exactly wrong. Different. It felt as if something were crawling around in his belly, and then he remembered the ants the frog had eaten. Were they inside of him, alive, somehow? He stood up and shook his head. His head was pounding, and then he realized that what he was hearing was his own heartbeat, and the crawling sensation was hunger. How could he be hungry again so soon? And yet, he was, hungrier than he'd ever felt. The crawling in his belly and the pounding in his head were almost too much to bear. All he could do was run.

As his body moved, the landscape behind the girl's house flew by, and eventually he was back at the pond where he had dragged himself the night before, so weak he could barely move. Now he had never felt so alive. And so, so, so hungry.

There were juicy-looking ducks in the pond, but they squawked and flapped their wings and took off as soon as they saw him. The squirrel was not so lucky. Its cheeks had been filled with nuts, and he soon outran it. The nuts added an interesting flavor to its head, he decided.

The crawling in his belly and the pounding in his head were gone — at least for now. Now he would take another nap, store up some energy until nightfall. Then it would be time to hunt again.

CHAPTER EIGHT

When I got home, Bert was right where I left him, under the rhododendron bush. Part of me wondered if he'd even moved since that morning. But then we found the headless squirrel. Danny filmed it from just about every angle while I watched Bert.

"Is he . . . dead?" Danny asked, peering over my shoulder with his phone.

"Do you have to film *everything*?" I asked.

"Pretty much," he said.

We both leaned in. Bert was lying very, very

still. But I could see his chest move up and down, faintly.

"Nah," I said. "Just napping."

"He must be tired, from all the hunting and killing," Danny said. "And, you know, from eating heads."

"It's natural for cats to nap during the day," I informed him. I looked down at Bert again. Even though his fur was still missing in places, the fur he did have looked shinier, and he didn't seem quite so skinny. "Is it just me, or does he already look a little bit better?"

Danny squinted. "I guess eating heads agrees with him."

"What are you two weirdos looking at?"

Danny and I turned around. It was Carl Weems. I could see where he'd thrown down his dirt bike in my yard. He lives the next street over from me, and he's always prowling around the neighborhood, sticking his nose where it doesn't belong.

"Nothing," I said. "Just a cat."

Carl stopped in his tracks when he saw Bert. He made a face.

"*That's* a cat?" he said.

"He's *sleeping*. Don't wake him up," I whispered.

"It looks like a pile of hamburger meat with fur on it," Carl said. And then he laughed, revealing his gray front tooth. Carl had flipped over his handlebars while trying to pop a wheelie last summer and had fallen face-first onto the sidewalk. His front tooth has never been the same.

"That's because he's a *zombie cat*," Danny said.

"Right," said Carl.

I gave Danny a look, but he kept going.

"He was dead when we found him, but Mellie brought him back to life. Now he only eats *brains*," he said, showing Carl the remains of the squirrel. "His name is . . . ZomBert."

Carl laughed again. "Nice try, Hurley," he said. "You can't fool me with your special effects. I bet the cat is fake, too. No cat could be that ugly."

Bert opened one pale-yellow eye. He looked right at Carl. Suddenly, Carl wasn't laughing anymore.

"Uh-oh," I said. "You've woken him up."

"Maybe ZomBert is hungry for dinner," Danny said. "Do you think he'd want Carl's brain?"

"That would be more of a *snack*," I said.

"You two and your freak cat can have one another," Carl said, backing away. Then he got on his bike and rode off.

"That was awesome," Danny said. He scratched Bert behind his good ear.

"ZomBert? Really?" I said.

"Hey, it worked on Carl," Danny reminded me. "And nothing I said was a lie. You did bring Bert back to life. Maybe not literally, but still. And he does like to eat animal heads. And he does look like a zombie. They're always skinny and nasty, with yellowy eyes and missing hair and body parts and stuff."

"Bert is not *nasty*," I said. "And he's not a zombie."

"Meeeeeow," said Bert. Maybe he wasn't nasty, but his breath definitely was.

"He'd be the perfect subject for my next film," Danny said. "If he'd, you know, actually *do* something."

Danny and I spent the next half hour trying to get Bert to play with us. But he just wanted to lie there in the shade.

"What's the matter?" I asked him. "Are you sick?"

"Some zombies only assume their full power at night," Danny said. "Maybe we should dig a hole for him to sleep in, so he can really be out of the sun."

"I'm not digging a *hole* for my cat to *sleep in*," I said.

"Fine," Danny said. "Then let's go to my place. I can show you more stuff about zombies and we can eat leftover pizza."

I shrugged. I was always happy to get away from the *Family, Food, and Fun* zone. And I do love pizza.

"I'm going to Danny's!" I called into the kitchen from the back door.

My mom waved. She and the twins were helping my dad unpack groceries.

"Okay!" she called back. "See you later!"

"What's this?" Emmett asked, pulling something out of a bag.

"That's a zucchini," my dad informed him.

"We're going to blog all about cooking with squash this week," my mom explained.

"Ookini! Ookini!" Ezra shouted, clapping his hands.

"Are you making zucchini cake?" I asked. Zucchini

cake is my favorite, especially the way my dad makes it, with chocolate chips.

"Among other things," said my dad. "Would you like to join us?"

"We made these *amazing* squash hats for our video," my mom said, pulling out four papier mâché monstrosities in different shades of green and orange and yellow. "We could make you one, too!"

"Uh . . . no thanks," I said. "Just save me a piece of cake."

I knelt next to Bert before Danny and I left.

"I, uh, just wanted to say thanks for sharing your frog this morning, and your squirrel this afternoon," I said. "That was really nice. I don't get very many warm meals these days, so I'm sure they would have been delicious, if I were, you know, into eating woodland creatures. Okay, I gotta go to Danny's. See you later. I hope."

Bert didn't open his eyes, but I had a feeling he heard me.

Unfortunately, when we got to the apartment where Danny and his mom live, he made me sit there while he went through his entire horror movie and book and comic book collection and showed me all the stuff about zombies. There was . . . a lot.

"Okay. First, zombies have grayish skin and yellowy eyes," Danny said. He opened a book called *Horror Show* and showed me several bookmarked pages of zombie movie photos. "Bert has grayish skin and yellowy eyes."

"But Bert has gray fur, so of course his skin is gray. And a lot of cats have yellow eyes," I informed him.

Danny grabbed a comic book called *Something Rotten in ZombieTown* and flipped through it. "Well, how about this: zombies suffer from decomposition. They're always losing body parts. Bert's missing part of his ear and some of his fur. And he does smell pretty rotten."

"He could have lost part of his ear in a catfight, and his fur already looks like it's starting to grow back. As for the smell, he was living in the *garbage* when we found him, remember?" I said. "Right now, only his breath smells bad. Maybe he just needs to have his teeth cleaned."

"Okay, well . . . zombies tend to shamble. Though

in some video games, like *Undead Planet* and *Virus Z,* they move pretty fast," Danny said.

We both shrugged. We hadn't seen Bert move very much at all.

"What about the fact that he eats *brains?*" I asked.

"I just said that to scare Carl," Danny admitted, looking for the TV remote. "The brain-eating thing is a common misconception. Zombies don't eat, since they're, you know, *dead.* They just like to bite their victims to infect them, so they can increase their horde."

When Danny finally found the remote control, we watched his favorite zombie movie, *Unstoppable Undead.* It's not a bad movie, actually; it's cool how it turns out that the zombie horde is being controlled by an evil mastermind. But the parts where they bite their victims are pretty gross. I plugged my ears so I didn't have to hear the *crunch-crunching* sounds.

And I had to admit, Danny was right. Something about all the zombies he showed me did remind me of Bert. But Bert was a real cat, and zombies were made up. Weren't they?

Danny's mom came home just as the movie was ending. She looked frazzled, as usual. When she put her work bag on the dining room table, just about everything inside spilled out.

"Hey, you," she said, giving Danny a kiss on the head. They'd grown extra close since Mr. Hurley left last year. It turned out he'd met some gross lady online and ran off to live with her in Florida. Danny doesn't like to talk about it, and I don't blame him.

Danny switched off *Unstoppable Undead* and put on regular TV. His mom tolerates his horror movies, but only if she doesn't have to watch them.

"Hi, Ms. Hurley," I said, waving.

"Hi, Mellie. How was school, kids?" she asked.

"No visible scarring," Danny said.

His mom tousled his hair as the YummCo jingle blared from the TV.

YummCo brings the fun-co!
The fun has just begun-co!
Be smart, not dumb-dumb-dumb-co!
And fill your day with YummCo!

At the end of the jingle, Stuart Yumm appeared. He was wearing a suit with his trademark green-and-brown striped tie, and he was smiling. Mr. Yumm is bald, with the exception of one patch of hair, which he has obviously dyed and grown long and winds around the top of his head, as if he thinks it will fool anyone. Danny and I think it looks like orange soft-serve ice cream.

"The fun has just begun-co!" Mr. Yumm exclaimed, giving the thumbs-up, before an announcer went on to list YummCo Foods' weekly specials.

"I hear that jingle all day at work. It's like I can't get away from it," Ms. Hurley said, rolling her eyes. She rummaged through everything that had fallen out of her bag. "By the way, everyone in the office was given these today to bring home. Can you put them up in the neighborhood?"

She handed us a roll of tape and a few of the green-and-brown flyers, which promised coupons at YummCo Foods if you brought your cat in to YummCo Animal Pals (our local animal clinic/shelter) to be examined. Mr. Yumm was pictured on the flyers, giving his trademark thumbs-up.

"Sure, Mom," Danny said. He shoved them into his backpack. Then he looked at me. "Maybe you can bring Bert," he suggested.

"Who's Bert?" Ms. Hurley asked.

"Just . . . a cat," I said.

"We found him in the trash," Danny explained. I gave him a look. I didn't want his mom to know about Bert; what if she told my parents?

"Well, just don't bring him in here. You know our landlord doesn't allow pets," his mother said, opening the refrigerator. "Now, who wants leftover pizza?"

When I got home, Bert was still sleeping under the rhododendron bush. I picked him up and brought him inside in my hoodie. My parents were helping the twins build a fort, so they didn't see us.

"Did you have fun at Danny's?" my mother called after me.

"Yep," I said, rushing up the stairs.

When we got to my room, I unzipped my hoodie and put Bert on the floor. I expected him to dash under the bed. Instead, he just looked at me.

"Meow."

I sat on the floor near him. Slowly, he made his way over to me. I put out my hand, and he rubbed the side of his head against my fingers.

"You're scent-marking. That's what *The Cat Book* calls it," I informed him. "You have sebaceous glands all over your mouth and chin and eyes, which you use to deposit scent. Does that mean you like me?"

I looked Bert in the eyes. In *The Cat Book*, it says that if a cat really likes you, they'll blink at you slowly. It's their version of kissing.

But Bert didn't blink at me. He just stared back, his eyes wide and zombie-yellow. Was he considering whether or not to bite me, so I could join his horde?

"Meow," he said.

I hoped that meant no.

CHAPTER NINE

*E*ven when he slept, he dreamed about hunting. And when he woke up, he was starving. If he went without food for too long, the crawling in his belly and the pounding in his head overcame him, and it felt as if the hunger itself might eat him alive.

He particularly enjoyed leaping into the air and catching low-flying birds. They were so surprised, they never knew what hit them until it was too late. One died just from fright, before he even got a chance to sink his claws and teeth into it. Its head still tasted delicious, though. He would save the rest for the girl. Someday, she might decide to try it, and then she would truly appreciate his generosity.

He spent time with her just as the sun went down, allowed her to run her gentle hands over his fur. Her kind wasn't always gentle, but she was. He liked the way she looked into his eyes as she talked to him. He trusted this girl, even though he knew he shouldn't. But he always let her know when their time together was done, and she always opened the window for him. She gave him his freedom, unlike the others.

Night after night, he hunted, and with each meal, he could feel his strength not just returning, but growing. He needed his strength for what would come next.

CHAPTER TEN

On Tuesday, Bert left three headless birds on our back porch.

On Wednesday, I found five headless mice.

On Thursday, Friday, and Saturday, I found two headless moles, a headless chipmunk, and a headless garter snake.

On Sunday, I found ten headless crickets. Each time, I managed to bury the evidence before my parents saw it. I hoped they wouldn't notice how lumpy our backyard had become.

"Meow," Bert would greet me in the morning from under the rhododendron bush. His fur was growing back and looking sleek, and he definitely didn't look scary-skinny anymore. His all-brain diet seemed to be working.

Each time he attempted to share his "feasts" with me, I made sure to thank him. I kept blinking at him, but he wouldn't blink back. I tried not to feel too disappointed. We were still family, I kept reminding myself, even if he didn't want to kiss me.

Monday was the first day of our organism reports. Since I picked number three, I had to give mine that day. But I was ready; I drew a picture of a cat on poster board and labeled all the body parts. Thanks to my phone, I had lots of pictures of cats from *The Cat Book*, and photos of Bert to share: sleeping under the rhododendron bush, sitting in my lap, and even scent marking against my fingers. And of course, I had all my cat facts.

When Danny and I got to school, we saw a bunch of kids crowded around Carl Weems. He was giving his report first that day, and I could see he was even more prepared than I was. He was holding a cage covered with skull-and-crossbones stickers, and inside the cage were two *actual* rats.

"Maybe I should have brought Bert?" I said as we locked up our bikes.

"He'd probably would've been asleep the whole time," Danny reminded me. He was probably right.

Other than the living visual aids, Carl's report wasn't all that great. He hardly had any facts about rats, other than what they ate (everything, apparently) and what their poop looked like. But it didn't matter; aside from me and Danny, everyone in class was fascinated.

"So, this is Chunk and Zoomer," Carl said. He opened the cage and took out the rats, holding one in each hand. They seemed pretty wriggly and twitchy, and their paws looked like tiny pink human hands. Their tails were long and hairless.

"Which one is which?" Marco Lanza asked.

"Chunk is the fat one, duh," Carl said. "But they both eat a lot."

"Can we hold them?" asked Will Gorton.

"Sure!" said Carl. But when he went to hand

Chunk and Zoomer to Will, Mr. James stopped him.

"I think it's best if we all observe these animals while they're in their cage," he said. "We wouldn't want anyone to drop them."

"Or contract the bubonic plague," Danny whispered to me.

Carl and the rest of the class seemed disappointed as he put the rats back in their cage and gave the latch on the cage door a little extra nudge to lock it in place. The rats looked out at all of us with their beady eyes. I was glad that was as close as I was going to get to them.

Owen Brown went next with his stegosaurus report. He didn't tell us anything I didn't already know about dinosaurs, but he did make a pretty cool diorama with a plastic stegosaurus and T. rex, and an action figure he'd dressed like a caveman. Mr. James gently reminded him that cavemen and dinosaurs never coexisted.

Carl snorted. "Looks like *Brown*'s diorama is a big fat *turd!*" he exclaimed.

"We're not always going to have the right answers," Mr. James informed the class. He clapped Owen on the shoulder before he sat down. "What's important is that we're all here to learn. Now, who's next?"

"Me," I said. I set up my notecards and my poster board with my cat diagram, and Danny helped me hook up my phone to the projector so I could start the slideshow I put together from the photos I took. But I didn't even get to start talking, because everyone in the class was laughing.

"What . . . is . . . that?" Nina Chen asked, pointing to the image of Bert projected on the screen.

"A cat," I said. I cleared my throat. "This report is about cats."

"My cat doesn't look like that," Nina said. "Felicity has both her ears. And all of her teeth and fur. And her eyes don't look . . . *evil*."

"That's because it's a zombie cat. They even call it ZomBert," Carl informed everyone. "It's way uglier in person, and it smells worse than garbage. It even eats *brains*."

"Many animals enjoy eating the heads of their prey," Mr. James said. "The head is very rich in nutrients."

"Eeeeeewwwwww . . . " It was as if the whole class was saying it at once.

"Okay, settle down," Mr. James said. "Like I said, we're all here to learn. So let's give Mellie our undivided attention."

But I didn't want everyone's undivided attention. I wanted to disappear.

"Cats are small, furry, carnivorous mammals," I began. I showed an image from *The Cat Book* of two kittens snuggling.

"They're not *all* furry," Carl muttered when I showed a photo of Bert curled up under the rhododendron bush.

Everyone started laughing again.

Somehow I managed to get through the rest of my report. While everyone snickered at my photos of Bert, I kept my eyes on my notecards and read them as fast as I could. When I was done, I rolled up my poster board and rushed back to my seat. "Good job," Danny whispered.

"A little rushed, Ms. Gore, but very informative," Mr. James said. "So . . . who's next?"

I was glad Danny was with me on the ride back to my house. He knew I didn't feel like talking, so he didn't say much, either. We just pedaled together in silence, our tires bumping over the cracks in the sidewalk.

"I keep forgetting to hang up those YummCo Animal Pals flyers my mom gave me," he said. "Want to help me?"

I nodded. I was glad for the distraction. We pulled over and Danny got the flyers out of his backpack; we started putting them up on telephone poles with the tape Ms. Hurley gave us. *It's nice of YummCo to support such a worthy cause,* I thought. Even though, technically, they owned the animal clinic, too. And the flyer was mainly a YummCo logo and a photo of Mr. Yumm giving his trademark thumbs-up.

"Maybe we *should* bring Bert there," I said. "The vet can check him out and make sure he's really okay."

"But how are we going to get him there?" Danny asked.

I thought for a minute. "I have a plan," I said.

An hour later, we were wheeling Bert through the neighborhood in the suitcase my parents bought me last year when we visited my grandparents in Michigan. I made sure to leave one corner zipped open, so Bert could get some air.

"He doesn't sound happy," Danny said.

"Well, no one likes going to the doctor," I said. "But trust me: this is for your own good, Bert."

Inside YummCo Animal Pals, the wallpaper and the furniture were brown and green. The YummCo jingle was playing softly in the background.

YummCo brings the fun-co!

The fun has just begun-co!

Be smart, not dumb-dumb-dumb-co!

And fill your day with YummCo!

"Look," said Danny. "It's actually him. The big man himself."

"Who?" I said.

I was almost too distracted by everything else to

notice that Stuart Yumm was standing there at the counter. He posed next to a bulletin board of cat photos, shaking the vet's hand as a photographer took their picture. He looked larger than life, with his fancy suit and brown-and-green striped tie, and his swirled orange hair looked even brighter in person. His daughter, Yolanda Yumm, was by his side.

"It's always *fun-co* to check in on one of my businesses," he said, giving a thumbs-up for the camera. "Especially one that's helping animals *and* the community."

"Yes, *such* fun-co," Yolanda cooed. Then she flipped her perfectly straight, shiny red hair and flashed her perfectly straight, white teeth as the photographer snapped away. My parents were always raving about her best-selling cookbook and her lifestyle blog, *Yumm Life*, where she talked about how she balanced being a glamorous celebrity and helping her father with his business empire. I wished I had that problem.

The only one who didn't seem impressed by it all was Bert. We were barely inside the clinic when he

started going crazy. I could barely hold on to the suitcase handle.

"Easy, boy," I said, trying to sound soothing. But Bert wasn't having any of it.

Mr. Yumm and Yolanda craned their necks.

"Did you hear that?" Yolanda asked.

"What?" asked Mr. Yumm.

"I thought I heard something. And now the door's open," she noted.

"Oh, that happens all the time," the vet explained. "Especially on windy days."

That was it. In a flash, Bert busted out of the suitcase and ran down the street.

"Aww, I wanted to get a photo with Mr. Yumm," Danny said. "There goes that idea."

We tried to catch up with Bert, but there was no sign of him. And then Carl was behind us on his bike. Chunk and Zoomer's cage was attached to his back fender with bungee cords.

"That was some presentation today, *Gore-eyes*," he said. "I nearly lost my lunch when you showed us those photos."

I didn't say anything, because I knew the more

attention Carl got, the more he'd bother us. Instead, I focused on getting as far away from him as possible, though it was hard to fast-walk while dragging the suitcase behind me. Danny did his best to keep up. Unfortunately, Carl was pedaling next to us before long.

"You think you're supersmart. But admit it — my report was awesome compared to yours."

"You didn't even give a report. You just waved your dumb rats around," Danny said.

"At least my rats are cute and fun," Carl said. "Not like her nasty zombie cat. It looks like it ate itself, and then threw up!"

"That doesn't even make any sense," Danny said.

"You don't make any sense," said Carl. "No one wants to be friends with you, except for a girl, *Girly Hurley!*"

"Shut up, Carl!" I shouted. "Shut up and go away!"

"MEEEEEEEEOOOOOOOOW."

It was Bert. He must have heard me yelling. He ran toward us. When he got to Carl's bike, and saw Chunk and Zoomer shifting around in their cage, he stopped and opened his mouth a tiny bit and sniffed. His vomeronasal organ must have been going crazy.

"Well, if it isn't *ZomBert*," Carl said. "I bet if I ran it over with my bike, it'd be an improvement."

"Don't," I said.

Carl rolled his bike forward.

"Cut it out!" Danny yelled. But Carl just laughed. He flashed his dead tooth. Then he put his feet up on the pedals. "Stop!" I cried.

"ROOOOOOOOOOWR," Bert growled, focusing his bright yellow eyes on Carl. He puffed up what little fur he had. His ears (well, what was left of them) flattened against his head. And then, he leaped.

"Bert! No!" I yelled. Danny almost dropped his phone, which he was using to record the whole thing.

The next few seconds were a blur. I dropped my suitcase and lunged forward. Bert hissed and flew at Carl's head, and Carl fell on the grass. His bike clattered to the pavement with Chunk and Zoomer still in their cage.

"My rats!" Carl cried. "Are you okay, boys?"

Carl opened the cage door and pulled out Chunk

and Zoomer and inspected them. They seemed okay,
though they were even more jittery than usual.

"Y-you'd better keep that demon cat away from
me *and* my rats," Carl said. He was pale and shaky,
but he still managed to get Chunk and Zoomer back
in their cage, get back on his bike, and ride away.

"He's not a demon cat, he's a *zombie* cat!" Danny
called after him.

As soon as I could catch my breath, I wanted to
make sure Bert was okay.

"Bert?" I called. But he was nowhere to be found. I ran around the back of the house and looked under the rhododendron bush, but he wasn't there, either.

"Maybe he's hiding. He's probably afraid," Danny said.

"Why would Bert be afraid?" I asked.

"You did yell pretty loud," he replied. "You kinda scared *me*, actually."

"Sorry," I said. But the one I really wanted to apologize to was Bert. I knew he was only trying to protect his family — though I had to wonder what would have happened if Carl hadn't jumped out of Bert's way at the last minute.

That night we had a thunderstorm. Just in case, I left my desk light on so Bert could find his way, and I left my bedroom window open a little bit, so I could hear if he was meowing for me to let him in. But all I saw were flashes of lightning, and all I heard as I fell asleep was the heavy patter of raindrops, the rumbling of thunder, and the howling wind. Wherever Bert was, I hoped he was safe and dry. And I really hoped he wasn't afraid.

CHAPTER ELEVEN

I thought your ploy with YummCo Animal Pals was going to bring me *results*," the Big Boss growled. "You know how much I *hate* photo ops."

"I was sure it would work," Kari said. It had been her idea to offer the free cat food coupons for the exam. If Y-91 was being cared for by someone in town, she figured they'd bring him in for proper care. But the vet had provided photos of every cat they'd treated, and there was no sign of him.

"It was definitely a long shot," Greg said. Kari glared at him.

"Well, what are you waiting for? Get the hazmat team back together!" boomed the Big Boss, banging a fist on the desk. "This time, scour the whole town — I want that thing back here, dead or alive!"

"A 'long shot'?" Kari said to Greg after they'd left the Big Boss's office. "Like you've had any better ideas. In fact, you haven't had any ideas *at all*."

Greg shrugged. "Maybe Y-91 really is dead," he said.

"Even if he is dead, we still need to find him," she reminded him. "There are all sorts of tests we need to run."

"Well, we're not going to find him tonight," Greg said, consulting his phone. "We're in for a big storm."

"We're in for a bigger storm if we don't find that thing," Kari said, motioning to the Big Boss's office. "For now, we need to get back to the lab. YummCo Animal Pals just sent us a new batch of strays, and they need to be processed and tagged. Even if Y-91 doesn't turn up, our work still continues."

"If Y-91 doesn't turn up, we might not even *have* jobs," said Greg.

"Speak for yourself," said Kari, sneering. "*I'm* not coming back from another search empty-handed."

CHAPTER TWELVE

By Tuesday morning, the storm had passed. Bert was still missing, and he hadn't left me any headless creatures. But I did find something else on our damp back porch. I showed it to Danny on the way to school.

"Is it a sticker?" he asked, running his finger over the skull and crossbones on it. "It looks familiar."

I nodded. "It's from Chunk and Zoomer's cage. Carl had these stickers all over it."

"Whoa," Danny said. "Bert means business."

"He was just defending us," I said. "Hopefully Carl will leave us alone from now on."

"He will, if he knows what's good for him," Danny said.

But as soon as we arrived at school, Carl was in my face.

"Chunk has been acting weird ever since your cat attacked us," he said. "If my rat turns into a zombie, you're in big trouble."

"If your rat turns into a zombie, we're *all* in big trouble," Danny said.

"Bert didn't even touch your rats," I said. Even though I didn't know that for sure. We couldn't see everything that happened during their run-in, even when Danny and I watched his video in slow motion. And Bert did get close enough to get that skull-and-crossbones sticker. Did he do something to Chunk? If he did, it would be all my fault.

"If Bert really wanted Chunk and Zoomer, they wouldn't have heads by now," Danny said.

All of the color left Carl's face.

"Just stay away from me, and stay away from my rats, if you know what's good for you," he managed to say as he backed away.

"Whoa. He seems really scared," I said.

"Bullies are the biggest wimps. It's a fact," Danny said.

All day, I wondered if Bert was going to come back, and if he was okay. But when I got home from school, he wasn't under the rhododendron bush. Danny and I walked around the block, calling for him and looking under shrubs and in our neighbors' garbage cans. It was hot and smelly work, and still, no Bert.

"What now?" I asked.

"You have all those photos of him on your phone," Danny reminded me. "Maybe we could make some Lost Pet signs and put them around the neighborhood."

"But we can't use my phone number on the signs, or my parents will find out," I said.

"We can't use mine, either. I'm not allowed to give out my number," Danny said. "But my mom never said anything about an e-mail address. I can make a new alias."

"Works for me." I sat on the curb and sighed. "Do you think Bert's gone for good?"

"I'm an expert on ghosts, zombies, vampires, and werewolves," Danny reminded me. "Cats are an alien species to me."

Though it seemed hopeless, we printed out some signs featuring our best photo of Bert along with Danny's new e-mail address, FindBert@yummail.com, and hung them around the neighborhood. When I got home, I did my best to wash up before dinner, but I just couldn't shake the garbage smell. In a way, it comforted me, because it reminded me of Bert.

My mom had just finished filming the spaghetti and meatballs (and my dad and the twins, who were wearing fake moustaches and waving little Italian flags) when the doorbell rang. It was Carl and his dad. Mr. Weems looked just like Carl, except bigger, and older, and bald. Both of them even wore the same scowl.

"I don't know if your daughter mentioned her run-in with my son yesterday," Mr. Weems said. "But now it seems one of Carl's rats is missing. We believe that your cat is the culprit."

"When I got home, Chunk was gone," Carl explained, sniffling. "There was blood in the cage, and the door was open."

"I don't understand," my father said.

"We don't have a cat," my mother said.

They looked at each other. Then they looked at me.

There was nothing left to do but come clean. I took a deep breath.

"His name is Bert," I said, finally. "I found him. He's been sleeping under the rhododendron bush. And he didn't hurt anyone! Well, maybe a couple of small animals and bugs around the neighborhood, but never anyone's pets. And he did defend me and Danny against Carl yesterday, but only because Carl was making fun of us. Danny even filmed it all—he has proof! Bert wouldn't hurt Chunk!"

The more I tried to defend Bert, the guiltier he sounded. My parents' eyes were wide. Carl sniffled some more and wiped his nose on his sleeve. Mr. Weems looked at my parents and scowled again.

"Go to your room," my mother said.

"But—" I said.

"*Right now,*" said my father.

I curled up on my bed and waited for my parents to finish talking to Carl and his dad. This was the most trouble I'd ever been in, and that was including the time I tried to give myself bangs when I was six.

Soon, there was a faint knocking at my door, and a familiar giggling.

"Mellie, we come in?" Emmett whispered.

"I guess so," I said. "I just can't come out."

Immediately, the twins scrambled up on my bed with me. We used to play in my room all the time, before my parents decided to make them viral video stars. That seemed like such a long time ago.

"Where your books? Where your fun art stuff?" Emmett asked.

"Where Mr. Peepers?" added Ezra.

"It's all . . . put away," I said. I didn't want to tell them about Mr. Peepers's gruesome beheading, along with all my other stuffed animals.

"Where the kitty?" asked Ezra.

"Hiding in here?" Emmett said, looking around.

"No," I said. "I don't know where he is."

"You going to *jail*?" Emmett asked, his eyes wide.

The twins liked to put all of their stuffed animals underneath an overturned laundry basket and call it jail. It was one of their favorite games.

"Probably not," I said. "But I am in a lot of trouble."

"Twubble! Twubble!" Ezra repeated, clapping his hands.

"It's not as fun as it sounds, kiddo," I said.

An hour went by. I could hear the twins running up and down the hall after their bath, as Mom and Dad attempted to get them into bed. I distracted myself by looking over my cat report. Mr. James was right; it was very informative. And my drawing of a cat wasn't half bad. I flipped through the photos on my phone, of Bert sleeping in my lap and rubbing against my fingers. Could he really have done something to Chunk?

When my parents finally came in, my mother's face was bright red, the way it gets when she's *really* angry, and my father wouldn't even look me in the eye. He just kept shaking his head. I needed to talk fast.

"I'm sorry I didn't tell you about Bert," I blurted. "But I was worried you'd say I couldn't keep him. He only stays in my room for a few hours after school, and he likes being out at night, so it's barely like having a pet at all. You guys didn't even notice, and it's been over a week!"

"You *lied* to us, Mellie," my dad said. "We trusted you."

"If you'd just look at these photos of him, you'd see how special he is," I said, holding out my phone.

"Mellie, that cat is not a pet. It's a feral animal," my mom said.

"But if you'd just look—" I tried to say.

"It could have attacked the twins!" my mom said, raising her voice. Her face was really red now. I noticed she didn't seem very worried about a feral animal attacking me.

"Things are going to have to change around here," my dad said, taking the phone from me.

"Your free-range days are *over*, young lady," my mom said. "From now on, you are coming straight home after school."

"But what about Danny?" I asked.

"You can spend time with Danny, but only here at our house, so we can keep an eye on you," Mom said.

I thought about all the fun stuff Danny and I did together on our own: our adventures all over Lambert, our projects and experiments, Danny's movies. Hanging out at his house and eating leftovers. All of the things we wouldn't be able to do in my boring house with my parents and the twins always around. But then I had another thought.

"What about Bert?" I asked.

"If we see that cat in the neighborhood again, we're going to have to call animal control," my mom said.

"In the meantime, you need to stay away from it," my dad said.

No. This couldn't be happening.

"But Bert would never hurt me! We like being together. And we look out for each other," I tried to explain. "It's like we're family."

"*We're* your family," my mother reminded me. "And we're looking out for you, too."

"And we like being with you," my dad added.

"Not unless I want to be on camera, which I *don't*!" I cried.

My parents looked at each other.

"We didn't realize you hated the blog so much," my father said.

"I don't hate it," I said. "It's just *all the time,* with all those costumes and props and songs."

"We thought you wanted some space. That's why we've been letting you go out on your own," my mother said.

"I know," I said. "I like doing my own thing, sometimes."

"Well, 'doing your own thing' doesn't mean you can just bring an animal into the house. Bert might seem nice to you, but he could be sick," my father said. He took my phone from my mom and starting flipping through the photos. "He looks like . . . he's been through a lot."

"He could have rabies, or some other disease that's not safe for him to be around people," my mother said. "Especially if he's been exhibiting aggressive behavior."

"Bert didn't do anything to Chunk," I said. The more I said it, the more I felt pretty sure it was true.

"Well, he did scare Carl enough to knock him off his bike," my father said. "And that's serious."

That was true. And if Carl didn't fall off his bike, Chunk and Zoomer's cage wouldn't have hit the ground. Maybe something happened to Chunk when he fell. Maybe when the cage hit the ground, it loosened the cage door.

"Oh," I said.

"The most important thing is for you to apologize to Carl," my father said.

"And then?" I said. "Can I go back to free-ranging?"

"We'll see," my mom said. "For now, work on *staying out of trouble*." They let me go downstairs after that to eat my spaghetti and meatballs, which I took as a promising sign.

That night I couldn't sleep. Usually I can make myself tired by reading, but leafing through *The Cat Book* just made things worse. All the photos of the cats in the book seemed nothing like Bert. They all looked normal and frisky and cute as they did normal cat things, like playing with balls of yarn or eating out of a cat bowl or stretching out on a sunny windowsill.

They weren't killing small animals and insects and eating their heads, or attacking boys . . . and possibly rats.

I remembered the way the other kids in class reacted that day during my presentation, when they saw my photos of Bert. If he didn't really look or act like a normal cat, maybe he wasn't.

Maybe Danny had been right all along. Maybe Bert was really . . . ZomBert.

And then I had the worst thought of all.

Maybe by rescuing Bert, and bringing him back to life, I'd unleashed a monster. Whatever he'd done to Chunk—and whatever he might do next—was all my fault.

That was it. I got out of bed and grabbed my jacket and my flashlight. I crept downstairs and out the back door, and then I got on my bike and started pedaling. I tried not to think about what Mom and Dad would do if they found out I'd left the house. Though they said my free-range *days* were over—they didn't say anything about going out at *night*. And anyway, I was on a mission, one I hoped they'd understand.

I'm going to find Bert, I thought. *And when I find him, I'm going to call YummCo Animal Pals, so they can bring him in. They'll know what's wrong with him . . . hopefully.*

I'd never been out so late before; it was colder than I thought it would be. I zipped up my hoodie to keep out the chill as I rode to Danny's. He and his mom live on the second floor of a three-family house. It took me a while to find the right-size pebbles, and to aim them so they'd hit his bedroom window. When I got my third bull's-eye, his light finally went on.

"Mellie?" he said, peering out. His hair was sticking up on one side and flat on the other.

"I need your help," I said. "I have to find Bert."

"Right now? What time is it?" he asked.

"Right now," I said. "Carl and his dad came over to my house tonight. Chunk is missing, and they're blaming Bert."

"What? Do you really think Bert did something to Chunk?" Danny asked.

"I don't know," I said. "But something isn't right about him."

"My mom will kill me," Danny said.

"And my parents will kill *me*. They've already grounded me and confiscated my phone because they don't trust me, for not telling them about Bert," I said. "But if he really is a zombie, it's my responsibility to bring him in."

Danny and I looked at each other. Finally, he nodded.

"I'll be out in five minutes," he said.

The streets of Lambert seemed quiet. Too quiet. All I could hear was the sound of my and Danny's pedaling. We checked around Danny's neighborhood, then mine, calling Bert's name and using our flashlights to inspect every potential hiding place. Then we went around our school and the high school and the town hall. No sign of Bert.

"Let's try the Green," Danny suggested.

The Green is the park at the center of town; Main Street cuts right through it. It was when we turned the corner onto Main Street that we saw them: brown-and-green YummCo delivery vans, all parked in front of the Super YummCo Superstore.

"They must be loading up for tomorrow's deliveries," Danny suggested.

And then we saw the lights. All across the Green, YummCo workers were walking with bright flashlights. At least, I assumed they were YummCo workers. They weren't wearing their trademark green-and-brown uniforms. Instead, they were wearing white coveralls with bright-green rubber gloves and boots, and their heads were covered with hooded breathing masks attached to oxygen tanks.

"Those are hazmat suits," Danny whispered. "As in 'hazardous materials.'"

"What do you think they're looking for?" I asked.

"Whatever it is, it isn't good," Danny replied.

"We should go," I whispered. Danny nodded, and we both turned back.

That's when I dropped my flashlight. It landed on the street with a clatter.

Suddenly, one of the workers' flashlights was on both of us, and everyone seemed to be looking our way. Two of them started coming toward us.

"Let's get out of here!" Danny shouted.

■ ■ ■

I didn't bother looking over my shoulder again. I knew they were after us; I heard the van's tires screeching, and then I saw the beam of its headlights. I don't know how I managed to pedal, I was so scared. When I finally turned around to look, the van was right on our tail. It was close enough that I could see the man and the woman in the front seat staring right at us.

"We should split up!" Danny shouted. "Meet back at my house!"

"Okay!" I shouted back, as he took a left past the pet store. I took a right. Unfortunately, the van was still following me, and I was headed right for the Super YummCo parking lot, where the rest of the hazmat crew was waiting. At the last minute, I turned so sharply I nearly fell off my bike. I pedaled through backstreets and into the town cemetery, where I jumped off my bike and hid it in some bushes. Then I crouched behind the biggest thing I could find, which was actually a monument to Nathaniel Lambert, the founder of our town. I stayed there for what seemed like hours, while I listened to the van driving around, looking for me.

That's when I saw what looked like a little gray shadow, slipping though the bars of the cemetery fence and heading toward the factory.

"Bert?" I whispered into the darkness. "Come here, boy! It's me, Mellie!"

In response, all I heard was the van, which sounded like it was driving away. Finally, I stood up and looked around. All was quiet again. Just past the cemetery was the YummCo factory; on the hilltop overlooking the factory and the rest of the town, I could see the dark outline of the Yumms' mansion. One window of the mansion was lit, like an open eye. I shuddered.

You really need to get a grip, I told myself. And I needed to get to Danny's. As I looked back at the mansion one last time, I could hear the faraway chiming of the clock at the Lambert town hall. It was midnight. That's when creepy things are supposed to happen, according to Danny. But I already had creepy things happening to me. They'd been happening ever since Bert entered my life. And now I was hiding in a cemetery in the middle of the night — could it get any creepier? I was afraid to find out.

Just to be safe, I waited another ten minutes before I pulled my bike out and rode to Danny's. I'd never been so grateful to see him sitting on the front steps of his building.

"I was just about to call the police," he admitted. "Are you all right?"

"I think so," I said. "Though my bike needs a *serious* cleaning."

"That was crazy," Danny said, shaking his head. "Do you think they saw our faces?"

"I looked at him. "Probably not. Bike helmets make everyone look the same." I said. "Why do you think they chased us?"

"Well, we *did* seem pretty suspicious," Danny noted. "And if something hazardous spilled out there, they wouldn't want anyone wandering around unprotected."

"I wonder if it has to do with the salmonella outbreak you heard about from your mom?" I said.

"I'll ask her tomorrow morning," said Danny, yawning. "If it does, it will be great for my presentation."

"You should probably go back to bed, so you don't fall asleep in the *middle* of your presentation," I said.

"True," Danny said. "I'll see you tomorrow. Sorry we didn't find Bert."

I was sorry we didn't find him, too. But the more I thought about it later, after I sneaked back into my house and into bed, the more I wondered if Bert just didn't *want* to be found. And if he was really a zombie, maybe it was better for everyone if he just stayed away.

CHAPTER THIRTEEN

The van screeched to a halt on a dark side street. Kari got out of the passenger seat and slammed the door. Greg followed suit.

"Ugh!" she said, throwing down her hazmat mask. "I can't believe you let them get away!"

"They were going pretty fast," Greg reminded her. "And it's much easier to navigate these streets on bikes."

"Wait till the Big Boss hears about this," Kari said. "You are *so* fired."

"Please don't say that I screwed up again. I really need this job," Greg pleaded.

"You've been a disaster at this job from the beginning. You just never saw the signs," Kari said, smirking.

Greg leaned against a tree and sighed. And then something beneath his hand crumpled. He looked down at the tree trunk, and at a piece of paper taped to it. When he pulled off the paper and got a closer look at it, his eyes widened.

"Hey," he said, showing it to Kari. "How's *this* for a sign?"

CHAPTER FOURTEEN

When I left for school the next morning, there were no "presents" waiting for me. Bert was still missing, I was exhausted, and my parents still seemed suspicious. If they only knew.

"So, you actually saw Bert—at the cemetery?" Danny asked.

"I don't know if I really saw him," I admitted. "It was dark. And I was tired. Not as tired as I am now, but still."

"I wish I had been in the cemetery with you," he said. "I would've had my phone. I could have gotten some *killer* footage."

I rolled my eyes. Leave it to Danny to think about turning my stressful situation into a horror movie.

"My mom said that the whole salmonella thing was cleaned up weeks ago," Danny informed me between yawns. "So there's no telling what those YummCo workers were doing out there, or why they'd chase us like that."

"And Bert still hasn't come back home." I said.

"Maybe he knew everyone was mad at him, for what he did to Chunk," Danny said.

"Everyone should be mad at *me*. It's all my fault," I explained. "I was the one who brought Bert home in the first place, and made him think I was his family. If I wasn't yelling at Carl, Bert wouldn't have thought I needed defending. And then he wouldn't have . . . done whatever he did to Chunk."

"If Carl wasn't being a jerk to us, you wouldn't have needed to yell at him," Danny pointed out.

"I should never have rescued Bert from that recycling barrel. What was I thinking?" I said. "Now he's on the loose. What if he tries to attack someone else? What if little animal brains aren't enough for him anymore? What if he's craving something . . . bigger?"

Danny squinted at me. "Did you get *any* sleep last night, Mellie? You have really dark circles under your eyes, and your voice sounds weird."

I stopped pedaling and looked at my reflection in the window of the YummCo Pet Store. I did look really awful. And then I had a terrible thought. I looked at Danny.

"What if *I'm* turning into a zombie, too?" I asked.

Danny grabbed me by the shoulders and looked me in the eyes.

"Have you been bitten by Bert, or by anyone or anything else lately?" he asked.

"No," I admitted.

He took off his Lambert Yumms baseball hat and leaned toward me. "Do you want to bite me?"

"No," I said, finally.

"Well," Danny said, "we'll have to monitor you closely over the next forty-eight hours, but I think you're fine."

That made me feel a little bit better, though I knew I'd feel a lot better when I could apologize to Carl. But it turned out he wasn't in school. When Mr. James noted his absence during morning roll call, I knew something was really wrong.

Was Carl sick? Was Chunk sick? Was Chunk a zombie? Was everyone in the Weems family now a zombie?

I spent the whole day with all of these questions spinning around in my brain. I couldn't even pay attention during Danny's salmonella presentation, even though it was just the combination of gross and interesting I usually like.

"It's too bad my mom couldn't get me real slides of salmonella bacteria from the YummCo Foods lab. My drawings just don't do them justice," Danny said as we rode home.

"Uh-huh," I said.

"If Bert really is a zombie cat, it's probably a good thing he wasn't taken to YummCo Animal Pals, where he could infect everyone," he said, pointing at one of the brown-and-green flyers we'd hung up the day before. "The last thing we need around here is an army of zombie pets."

"Mmm," I said.

"Earth to Mellie," Danny said, snapping his fingers. "Are you even listening?"

"Sorry, I've gotta go," I said. "There's something I have to do!"

"Aren't you supposed to go straight home after school?" Danny yelled after me.

But I didn't have time to answer. I pedaled as fast as I could, and I didn't stop until I got to the Weems's house. It seemed quiet; I hoped that was because no one was home from work yet, and not because Bert had already gotten to them. I took my chances and rang the doorbell.

For a while, nothing happened. And then the door opened.

Standing there was a woman. Her face and hands and clothes were splattered with something sticky and shiny . . . and red.

"Aaah!" I said, jumping back.

"Oh, dear!" she said, looking down at herself. "I must be a sight. Sorry I didn't hear you ring at first—I was back in my crafting room, varnishing a chair."

"Hi," I said. I took a second to catch my breath. "Um . . . is Carl home?"

Her eyes widened. "You're here to see Carl?"

"Why?" I asked. "Is he all right?"

"He's fine," she said. "Are you . . . a friend of his?"

"From school," I explained.

"Well, isn't that wonderful?" she clapped her hands together. "Carl! Someone is here to see you — a *friend*, from *school*!"

After a couple of minutes, Carl padded down the stairs. He was wearing sweatpants and no shoes and his hair was kind of messed up, but at least he wasn't a zombie. His eyes narrowed when he saw me in the doorway.

"I'll leave you two to talk about school things," his mother said. "Let me know if you want me to fix you a snack!"

"What are *you* doing here?" he asked, after his mom had gone back to her crafting.

"I — I came to see how you were," I said.

"I'm fine," Carl said. "Why wouldn't I be?"

"Well, you weren't at school today," I explained. "And, um, I also wanted to apologize. For the thing with Bert the other day. I'm sorry that you fell off your bike. And I hope Chunk and Zoomer are okay."

"They're fine, too," Carl said.

"*They* are? So, you found Chunk? Is he all right?" I asked.

"Sort of," Carl said. His eyes drifted upstairs, then back to me. "You wanna see?"

I wasn't sure I did, but I followed him anyway. What did he mean by "sort of"?

I'd never been inside Carl's house. It was very quiet, unlike our house, and it smelled nice, like flowers. Carl led me into his room. His curtains and sheets had rocket ships on them, and there were stars all over his ceiling.

"I didn't know you liked outer space," I said.

"My mom did all this, when I was little," he explained. "But yeah, I still think space is pretty cool."

"It is cool," I said.

"Squeak-squeak-squeak!"

The noise was coming from one of the cages next to Carl's bed.

"Why do you have two cages now?" I asked.

"Look," he said, pointing.

I peered into the cages. Zoomer was in the old cage with the skull-and-crossbones stickers all over it, and he was running around frantically. Chunk was in the other cage. But he wasn't alone. There was something pink and gray and shiny and lumpy with him.

"Is that . . . a *brain*?" I cried.

"Duh," said Carl. "It's *babies*."

I blinked, looking closer at the cage.

"But . . . Chunk is a boy rat," I said.

"Evidently not," Carl said. "That's why Chunk was so fat. She was already pregnant when we got her from the pet store. I guess she was ready to have her babies the other day, and busted out of the cage. We found her under our back porch this morning, along with all these little guys. Aren't they cute?"

I looked at the hairless gray-and-pink babies all around Chunk. Their eyes hadn't even opened yet. *Cute* was not a word I would use to describe them. Piled together like that, they really did look like a brain.

I exhaled.

"That's great," I said. "I'm glad everyone is okay."

"My mom let me stay home so I could watch them today. She called it my paternity leave," Carl explained.

"More like *rat*-ernity leave," I said.

"Ha-ha," Carl said. "So, um, I'm sorry I blamed ZomBert—I mean, Bert. I was just worried."

"I know," I said. "Actually, I was, too."

Carl and I stood there and looked at the rat babies for a few more minutes. And that's when it struck me: even though everyone laughed at Carl's mean, dumb jokes at school, he didn't have any real friends. Everyone was too scared of him, except for me and Danny. The only time I ever saw him around the neighborhood was when he was pestering us. Could Carl Weems, aka our archnemesis, actually be . . . lonely?

Finally, I cleared my throat. "So, do you want to hang out sometime? Since you like outer space, maybe you and Danny and I could go to the planetarium," I said.

For a second, I thought Carl was about to smile. But then he wrinkled his nose.

"And be seen with the *Weirdo Twins*? Uh, no thanks," he said.

"Oooookay," I said. "Well, I'm going to go now. Bye."

"Yeah, bye," Carl said. He didn't even look at me; he was sticking his fingers through the cage bars, making kissy noises at Chunk and her babies.

As I rode home, part of me was hurt that Carl would never see me and Danny as anything other than the Weirdo Twins. But another part of me felt worse for Carl. Deep down, I think he really did want to go to the planetarium.

When I got home, Danny was sitting on my front stoop.

"What's wrong?" I said.

"I was going to ask you that. The way you ran off, I thought you really were turning into a zombie," Danny said. "Where did you go?"

I got off my bike and sat down with Danny and told him the whole story about Carl and Chunk and Zoomer and the babies. And how I apologized to Carl and he apologized to me. When I got to the description of Carl's outer space–themed bedroom, Danny started laughing. His laugh sounds like a squirrel inhaling helium, so I couldn't help laughing, too.

"So Carl Weems is a secret space nerd," Danny said. "Not so secret anymore, though."

"I'm not going to tell anyone. I'm sure he'll reveal his true self when he's ready," I said.

"It's a bummer about Bert, though," Danny said. "I have to admit, I kind of hoped he'd turned Chunk into a zombie. That would have been so cool."

"*So cool?* Maybe in a movie or a comic book. Not cool *at all* in real life," I noted.

"You're probably right," Danny said. "So, if Bert isn't a zombie cat, what's the deal with eating animal heads, and those yellow eyes, and that missing ear, and how his fur was all patchy?"

"I don't know," I admitted. "And if Bert doesn't come back, maybe we'll never know."

"I hope that's not true, but if it is, I'll miss him," Danny said. "I liked that Bert wasn't normal. Normal is boring."

"True," I said.

Danny checked his watch. "Hey, I gotta go. It's Wednesday, so Mom and I are ordering Chinese."

I gave Danny a nod. I know Chinese food is his favorite, and he knows I know.

"See you tomorrow," I said. "Hey, do you want to go to the planetarium this weekend? I can see if my parents will take us, since I'm still not allowed to free-range."

"Sure," Danny said. "Do you want to help me edit my movie this weekend, too? I can probably bring everything I need over to your house. I want to combine the *Gone Ghoul* footage with the footage I took of Bert. I'm thinking of renaming it *Rise of ZomBert*."

I sighed. "Sounds like a winner," I said.

CHAPTER FIFTEEN

He stared at the lab on the other side of the fence. He'd been coming here each night, cutting through the cemetery and then standing on this spot, staring and thinking.

It had been just over a week since he'd found his freedom, but it seemed like forever. All that time, he remembered his promise to the others: he would come back for them. But now, the hole in the fence had been patched, and the chain link pulsed with a new energy. It was electrified, he could tell. He knew getting back in wouldn't be easy, but this was an unexpected challenge.

Then again, he wasn't the same weak, bloodied animal who'd passed out in a barrel of garbage. Now, he was . . . different. And now he had help — from the girl with the gentle hands, and the curious boy. Whatever the challenges might be, he felt ready. He would fulfill his promise to the others and rescue them. And he would fulfill his promise to himself, and exact revenge.

But first, there was something he needed to do.

CHAPTER SIXTEEN

For the next two days, Bert still wasn't under the rhododendron bush. All I could do was wonder where he was and if he was okay.

"What's the matter, Mellie-Mel? You haven't touched your lasagna," my mom said at dinner.

"I made it with extra cheese," my father pointed out. "Just the way you like it."

It *was* just the way I like it. And it was warm. A couple of days before, my parents had made a new rule: no cameras, costumes, or props at the table. It felt nice to have us all focused on the food and one another. It was like we were a real family again, instead of an ad for *Family, Food, and Fun*.

Too bad I still had other things to worry about. Well, one thing in particular.

"I was just thinking about Bert," I said.

"Well," my mom said, "your father and I have discussed it, and now that we know Bert actually didn't harm Carl's rat, we're considering letting you keep him, when and if he comes back around."

"But *only* if you take him to the vet and make sure he's healthy," my father added.

"Okay," I said. I pushed a bite of lasagna around with my fork.

"We thought you'd be happy," my father said.

"I am happy," I said. And I was, a little bit. It was great to know that I could keep Bert. But I wasn't sure I'd ever see him again. And if I did, would he even want to be my pet, after the way I'd yelled at him—and how I'd assumed he'd gone on a zombie rampage?

I managed to eat a few bites of lasagna, enough that I could be excused from the table, and I went to my room. I distracted myself by straightening and cleaning. I set aside *The Cat Book*; maybe tomorrow after the planetarium, Danny and I could go to the library so I could return it. I put all of the YummCo Organic Kitty Superfood I bought in a bag, which I decided to donate to YummCo Animal Pals. And then I lay down on my bed and tried to read a different book, one of my old favorites, about a girl and her brother who time travel. I knew how it was going to end, so it wasn't long before I fell asleep. I dreamed about being chased through time by giant rats and headless frogs.

When I woke up on Saturday morning, I was glad to be in my own bed, with no rats or frogs in sight. The sun was shining, and it looked like it was going to be a beautiful day. I ate my cereal while my parents attempted to feed the twins.

"Hey," I said. "Danny and I were thinking of going to the planetarium today. I know I'm grounded, but I was hoping it would be okay, if maybe we all go together?"

"Do you want to go to the planetarium and look at the stars and planets?" Mom asked Emmett and Ezra.

"Stars!" shouted Emmett, dribbling a fistful of oatmeal back into his bowl.

"Pwanets!" yelled Ezra.

"That sounds like a yes," my mother said.

"They don't allow cameras in the planetarium," I warned them.

"I *think* we'll survive," said Mom.

"In fact, I think we're going to have a *stellar* time," my father said, giving me a wink.

"Ooh, 'A Stellar Time' would make a great title for a blog entry!" Mom exclaimed. I rolled my eyes. Some things never change, I guess.

I got dressed after breakfast and went outside to wait while my parents got the twins ready. That's when I heard it.

"Meeeeeow."

And then I saw it.

Our backyard was covered with dragonflies, at least a dozen of them, their wings glittering in the sun. I didn't need to look too closely to know that none of the dragonflies had heads. Because there, sitting under the rhododendron bush, was Bert.

"You came back," I said.

"Meeeeeow."

I ran over to him and knelt down. "Thank you for the dragonflies," I said. "They're beautiful . . . in a way. It must have taken you forever to catch all of them. Is that why you've been gone for so long?"

"Meow."

He was probably down by the stream in the woods behind my house the whole time, I realized. It was always buzzing with dragonflies there.

"I'm sorry I believed Carl. I know you're not a zombie cat. You're just . . . different. And different is more than okay with me."

Bert pushed his head into my hand and rubbed against my fingers, purring.

"I know you have secrets," I whispered. "Someday, I hope I'll know some of them."

When Bert shifted, I noticed something underneath him: it was one of the YummCo Animal Pals flyers. Well, some of it, at least; the photo of Mr. Yumm was ripped so he was missing his head.

I turned to Bert, and his yellow eyes seemed to look right into mine. And then, slowly, he blinked.

CHAPTER SEVENTEEN

*S*o, let me get this straight," said the Big Boss. "Not only have you two *still* not located Y-91, you also didn't manage to apprehend the suspects you saw on the Green?"

"They were on bikes," Greg tried to explain. "They rode pretty fast."

"It looked like they were kids, anyway. I assume they were just out pulling pranks," Kari said.

"Assume nothing," said the Big Boss. "*I* assumed you two wouldn't fail me. I was wrong. And I *hate* being wrong."

"Well, we didn't fail completely," Greg said, putting a green file on the desk.

"What's this?" asked the Big Boss.

"It's a Lost Pet sign. While we were out searching, I found it taped to a tree in the neighborhood near the woods," Greg explained.

"I've already traced the e-mail address at the bottom, and you wouldn't believe who it belongs to," said Kari. "Roxanne Hurley—one of the secretaries *here*. The one who was asking about the salmonella outbreak the other day."

"Well, I guess there's use for you two yet," the Big Boss said, smiling.

Kari folded her hands in her lap primly. She smiled, too.

"Would you excuse us, Kari?" the Big Boss said.

"What?" Kari asked.

"I need to talk something over with Greg. A very exciting opportunity," the Big Boss explained.

"Oh. Okay," said Kari. "Of—of course."

Greg? Kari thought, as she left the office. *Why does he get an exciting opportunity? Finding that sign on the tree was just dumb luck. Emphasis on the dumb.*

She turned around and saw the office door closing slowly, the Big Boss and Greg still talking. Without her.

"You won't want to pass this up, Greg," the Big Boss was saying. *"Believe me."*

"Sounds like . . . fun," Greg said.

"Indeed," said the Big Boss, stroking the photo on the Lost Pet sign. "The fun has just begun-co."